A Name for Kitty

written by *Marcia Trimble*   illustrated by *Gloria Lapuyade*

Images Press – Los Altos Hills, California

Published by Images Press

Publisher's Cataloging-in-Publication
(Provided by Quality Books, Inc.)

Trimble, Marcia.
    A name for kitty / written by Marcia Trimble ;
illustrated by Gloria Lapuyade. -- 1st ed.
    p. cm.
    LCCN: 99-97128
    ISBN: 1-891577-63-8 (hbk)
    ISBN: 1-891577-64-6 (pbk)
    SUMMARY: Malinda Martha takes a kitten home from
the petshop and has a memorable experience finding a name
that sticks.

    1. Kittens--Juvenile fiction. 2. Names--Juvenile
fiction.   I. Lapuyade, Gloria.   II. Title.

PZ7.T7352Na 2000   [E]
                    QBI99-1863

    10 9 8 7 6 5 4 3 2 1

Text was set in Century Gothic.
Book design by MontiGraphics

Printed in Hong Kong by South China Printing Co. (1988) Ltd. on acid free paper. ∞

To cat lovers everywhere and to their kitty stories, too.   ~M.T.

To my children...Nicole, Colin, Roxanne, and Christopher.   ~G.L.

Malinda Martha

loved to go to the pet shop.

She ran inside to explore the sights and sounds.
The bell on the door jingled a welcome.

Sal held on to the shopping list as Malinda Martha
turned to investigate a tiny meow.

"Oh! Look at the kittens.
A little black and white kitten!" she exclaimed.

"May I take Kitty home?" she pleaded.
"We'll see," is all that Mother would say.

Mother and Malinda Martha drove off...
with food for big dog Duffy...but without
the black and white kitten.

Malinda Martha thought about Kitty all afternoon.

She wanted to see Kitty again.

Malinda Martha wriggled
and squirmed at every stop sign.
She didn't say a word. But
her heart was pounding, go, go, go.

Go!

One minute her heart was pounding...

and the next minute her heart was skipping a beat
as she ran to the black and white kitten...waiting...all alone.

And then her heart beat faster... with joy.
"Oh, Kitty waited! Kitty waited for me!" she said.

Sal set
Kitty up
in style...

cans of soft food, vitamins, a pillow, and toys.
Malinda Martha added a fleacomb!
And...a name tag!

On the way home, Kitty purred and purred.

Kitty played in Malinda Martha's room...
safe from big dog Duffy. Malinda Martha
tried out a different name for Kitty every day while...

Kitty zoomed around the room.
He was a ball of energy.

But sometimes Kitty froze in his own tracks.

And sometimes silly Kitty was afraid of his own shadow.

And sometimes
Kitty caught a catnap
in his very own catnip patch. Sweet dreams, Kitty!

If only Kitty could say his own little bit.
Would he choose Blackbeard as the perfect fit?
"Meow," he would cry. "A landlubber I am.
Meow! Meow! Just call me Sam."

Kitty would have to grow into a name that fit.

In time Kitty did grow up...independent...
but still cautious of big dog Duffy...

a tree climber...

a cat on the roof...

a field cat...

a cat who came to dinner...

as the perfect gentlecat
he had become.

Kitty had grown into a name that fit.
He had grown into
Sammy Sophisticat.

But he answered to just plain Sammy... the name that stuck!

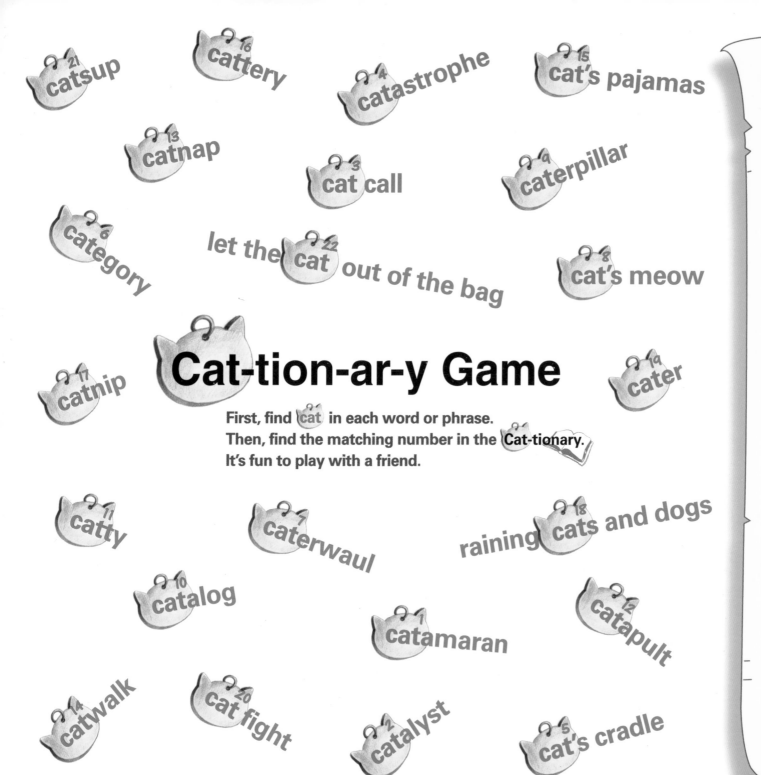

21 catsup
16 cattery
4 catastrophe
15 cat's pajamas

13 catnap
3 cat call
9 caterpillar

6 category
let the 22 cat out of the bag
8 cat's meow

Cat-tion-ar-y Game

17 catnip

19 cater

First, find cat in each word or phrase.
Then, find the matching number in the Cat-tionary.
It's fun to play with a friend.

11 catty
7 caterwaul
18 raining cats and dogs

10 catalog

1 catamaran

12 catapult

14 catwalk
20 cat fight
2 catalyst
5 cat's cradle

Cat-tionary

1. boat
2. change
3. cry
4. disaster
5. game
6. group
7. howl
8. image
9. larva
10. list
11. mean
12. move
13. nap
14. narrow walkway
15. outstanding
16. place
17. plant
18. pouring
19. provide food
20. quarrel
21. sauce
22. tell